The Secret Life of
SQUIRRELS

Nancy Rose

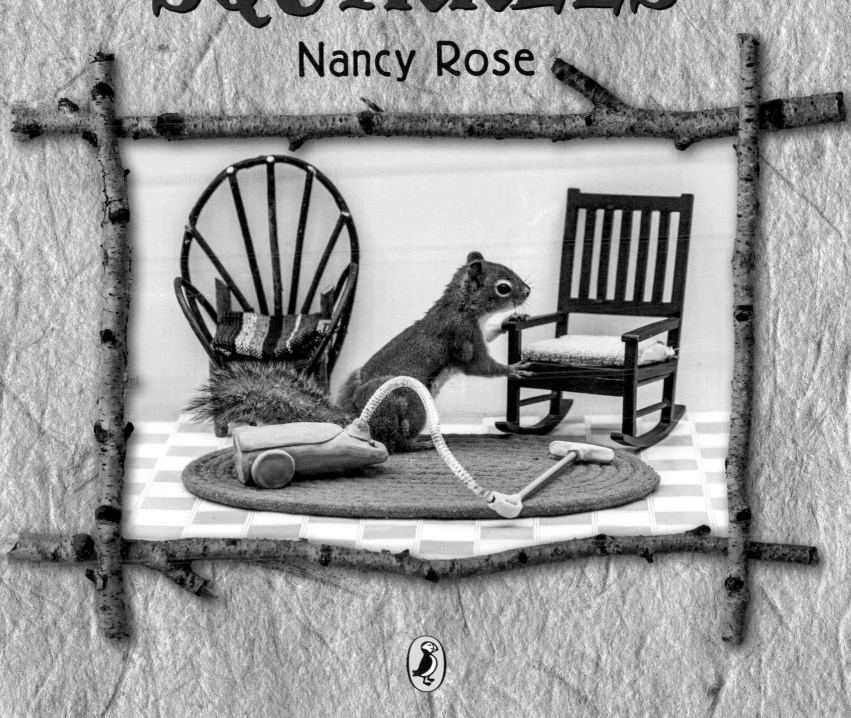

Mr. Peanuts

Most squirrels spend their days
gathering nuts and climbing trees.
Not Mr. Peanuts.
He is a rather unusual squirrel.

Mr. Peanuts
enjoys activities such
as cooking on his tiny grill.
(His hot dogs are
delicious.)

Mr. Peanuts plays the piano beautifully.
His favourite piece is *Moonlight Sonutta*.

Most squirrels would find that piece quite difficult to play.
(But then again, most squirrels don't play the piano.)

Mr. Peanuts likes to read. His favourite books are *A Tail of Two Cities* and *Good Night, Nut*. He especially likes to read aloud. (You may have heard him chattering in your backyard.)

Mr. Peanuts has a busy and mostly happy life.
But once in a while, he feels lonely.

Being a clever squirrel, Mr. Peanuts has an idea.
He sits down and writes a letter using his very
best penmanship:

MR. PEANUTS

Dear Cousin Squirrel,

Please come for a visit. I promise
you will have an excellent time.

Sincerely,
Mr. Peanuts

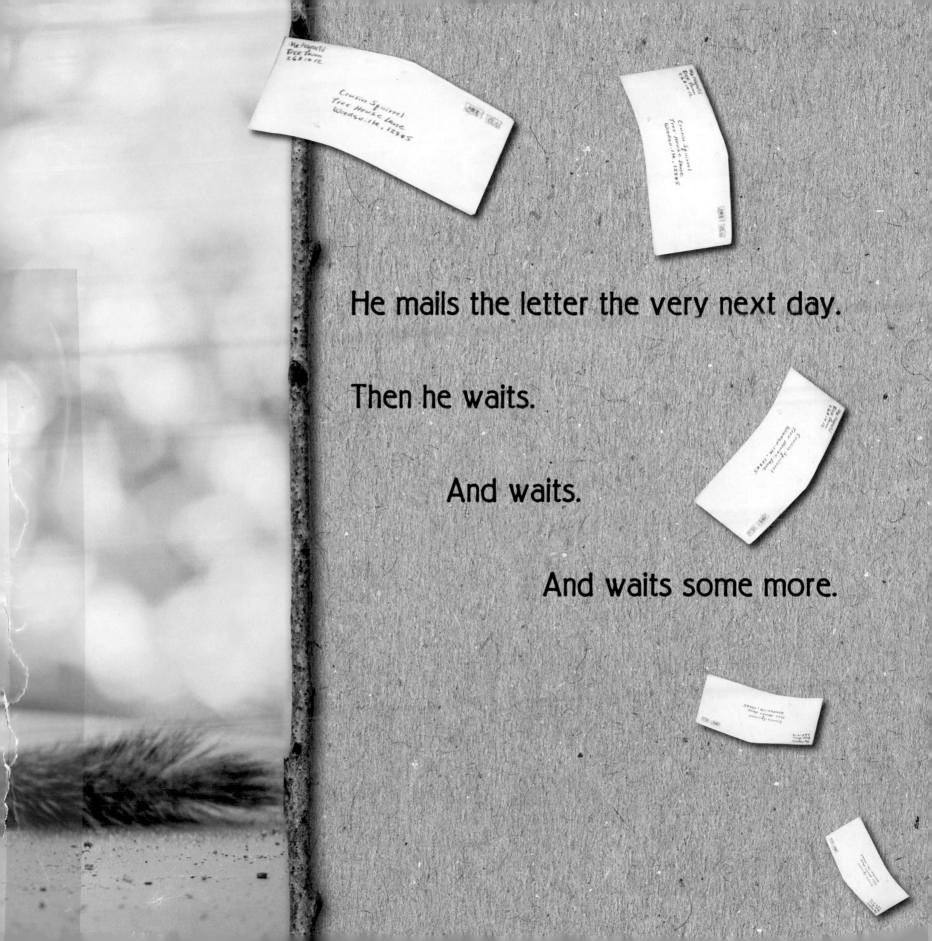

He mails the letter the very next day.

Then he waits.

And waits.

And waits some more.

He checks his mailbox every day, hoping for a reply. One day he finds a letter waiting for him. It reads:

Dear Mr. Peanuts, my favourite cuz,

Thanks for the letter. It's been too long. Can't wait to see what you're up to these days. I'll be there soon.
Cheers,
Cousin Squirrel

Mr. Peanuts smiles as he reads the tiny letter over and over. Then he gets right to work. He wants to make sure everything is perfect for his cousin's visit.

Mr. Peanuts dusts and cleans.
He even vacuums under the rug.

He does laundry, chattering to himself as he works. He is the tidiest squirrel around (and certainly the only one with a washer and dryer).

Mr. Peanuts makes up his cousin's bed just so, with the sheets tucked in tight. He wants him to have a great night's sleep.

Mr. Peanuts takes a bath with his rubber duckie.
(A squirrel can never be too clean.)

Finally, Cousin Squirrel arrives! He is
just in time for breakfast. Mr. Peanuts
and Cousin Squirrel both love pancakes.

Later, the two squirrels go for a wagon ride.
Mr. Peanuts soon learns that two squirrels
travel faster than one!

Mr. Peanuts teaches Cousin Squirrel how to play chess. Cousin Squirrel learns quickly. *It is more fun to play chess with a friend,* thinks Mr. Peanuts, *even if you don't always win.*

It is a beautiful day, so they pack a picnic.
Cousin Squirrel makes his peanut butter sandwiches
with an extra layer of crunchy peanuts. Mr. Peanuts
has never thought to try that. It tastes scrumptious.

That night, they build a campfire and scare each other with ghost stories, including "The Old Haunted Tree" and "The One-Eyed Owl." *You can't tell yourself a ghost story*, thinks Mr. Peanuts. *You need a friend.*

The next day, they go out for ice cream.
Mr. Peanuts has his usual scoop of peanut brittle.
Cousin Squirrel tries the flavour of the month:
buttery salted pecan.

Mr. Peanuts and Cousin Squirrel
are two rather unusual squirrels
who have a wonderful time together.

Having a friend
makes everything
twice as fun.

TEN TIPS FOR PHOTOGRAPHING WILDLIFE

1. Practise using your camera on things that do not move, like flowers, food—even a friend who can sit still!

2. Then practise on your pet. Try getting down to the animal's level for better close-ups. You may have to sit or lie on the ground.

3. Try to capture the animal's personality. Catch your pet being funny, playing with its favourite toy, or cuddling with its owners.

4. Keep your camera steady! You can rest your camera on something solid or use a tripod, which is a special camera stand.

5. Look for good light. The best days for photographing outside are bright, overcast days.

6. Action shots are always more interesting! Some cameras have settings for "sports," which will help you capture moving animals.

7. Take lots and lots and lots of shots.
8. Set up a feeding station for squirrels and birds in your yard if you can. The feeding station can be a bird feeder or just a small table with birdseed, as well as sunflower seeds and peanuts for squirrels.

9. Respect wildlife and be safe. For example, taking pictures of birds' nests might frighten the parents away, and they may not come back to their babies. Always be careful around pets and animals that you do not know. It is always best to have a parent or an older friend with you.
10. Finally, be PATIENT. You cannot ask a wild animal to pose for you.

While many animals are friendly, you can never be sure.
Please speak to an adult before photographing, approaching, or feeding an animal you do not know.

Q&A WITH NANCY ROSE

Q: How long have you been a photographer?
A: I owned my first 35-millimetre film camera when I was in my early twenties, and it wasn't until I bought a digital camera in 2007 that I really got into photography.

Q: Did you start with other subjects before squirrels?
A: My first subjects were mostly sunsets and flowers in my garden, which were much easier to shoot than squirrels since they don't move. I also loved taking photos on vacations and started bringing my camera with me almost everywhere I went.

Q: Why do you enjoy photographing squirrels in particular?
A: I love the curiosity of squirrels. When they started to become regular visitors to my bird feeders, I began taking photos of them, but you can only take so many similar photos of squirrels on a bird feeder before coming up with something new.

Q: What was in your first miniature photo shoot?
A: A mailbox made of red bristol board and some pieces of wood from the basement. It was such a big hit on Flickr that it inspired me to try more miniatures. That same photo ultimately inspired this book! I make most of my own props, like the miniature grill, which I built with foil pans and Popsicle sticks, and a bed made from tree branches.

Q: How many squirrels do you work with on your shoots?
A: Mr. Peanuts was my first "actor," but there have been three or four other little squirrels (Nicky, Pisa, and Claus) who came to visit now and then, and recently Mittens and another little female are the ones who come most often.

Painting the backdrop

Setting out the peanuts

Here comes the squirrel!

Q: How do you get the squirrels to pose?
A: Squirrels are curious creatures. They will inspect and explore anything if peanuts are involved, so I hide peanuts in and around my props.

Q: Would you describe the little photo studio setup on the railing of your back deck?
A: When the deck railing wasn't wide enough to hold my little props, I screwed a piece of plywood to the railing and added a backboard made from a piece of wire shelving. I can drape a piece of heavy plastic over it or stand a piece of painted foam board against it to be a "wall" in my scene. I usually have to clip things on or the wind will blow everything over. Sometimes I use my picnic table, too, and have two different sets on the go at once.

Q: How long does a photo shoot take?
A: Sometimes I spend a whole weekend waiting, and nothing happens. But if Mr. Peanuts or any of his friends are hungry, they'll come back quite a few times. Still, it might take thirty pictures to get a good shot. Squirrels move quickly! In a few cases I have taken over a hundred photos trying to get just the right one. The light is always changing, too, which makes it extra challenging. I process my photos on my laptop at my kitchen table, so I can always see when a squirrel comes on the deck, and my camera is on a tripod, so it is ready when I need it.

I go through a lot of peanuts because the blue jays usually beat the squirrels to the nuts!

PUFFIN

an imprint of Penguin Canada Books Inc., a Penguin Random House Company

Published by the Penguin Group

Penguin Canada Books Inc., 90 Eglinton Avenue East, Suite 700, Toronto, Ontario, Canada
M4P 2Y3

Penguin Group (USA) LLC, 375 Hudson Street, New York, New York 10014, U.S.A.
Penguin Books Ltd, 80 Strand, London WC2R 0RL, England
Penguin Ireland, 25 St Stephen's Green, Dublin 2, Ireland (a division of Penguin Books Ltd)
Penguin Group (Australia), 707 Collins Street, Melbourne, Victoria 3008, Australia (a division of Pearson Australia Group Pty Ltd)
Penguin Books India Pvt Ltd, 11 Community Centre, Panchsheel Park, New Delhi – 110 017, India
Penguin Group (NZ), 67 Apollo Drive, Rosedale, Auckland 0632, New Zealand (a division of Pearson New Zealand Ltd)
Penguin Books (South Africa) (Pty) Ltd, 24 Sturdee Avenue, Rosebank, Johannesburg 2196, South Africa

Penguin Books Ltd, Registered Offices: 80 Strand, London WC2R 0RL, England

Published in Puffin hardcover by Penguin Canada Books Inc., 2014
Simultaneously published in the United States by Little, Brown and Company, a division of Hachette Book Group, Inc., 1290 Avenue of the Americas,
New York, NY 10019

1 2 3 4 5 6 7 8 9 10 (RRD)

Copyright © Nancy Rose, 2014

Manufactured in Mexico

Library and Archives Canada Cataloguing in Publication

Rose, Nancy, 1954-, author, photographer
The secret life of squirrels / Nancy Rose.
ISBN 978-0-670-06822-7 (bound)
I. Title.
PS8635.O6463S42 2014   jC813'.6   C2014-904164-0

eBook ISBN 978-0-14-319311-1

Visit the Penguin Canada website at www.penguin.ca

Special and corporate bulk purchase rates available; please see www.penguin.ca/corporatesales or call 1-800-810-3104.

Photo credits:
Jacket front flap, back flap, 7, 12 (wood grain): Maxim Tupikov/shutterstock.com • Jacket front flap, spine, 2–3, 32 (nuts): Cora Mueller/shutterstock.com
• Jacket spine, back cover, 1, 9, 11, 19, 21, 22, 24, 28–29, 32 (handmade paper): Taigi/shutterstock.com • Jacket back cover, 20 (fabric with embroidery): Natal.T/shutterstock.com • Jacket back cover, back flap, 1, 4, 6, 7, 8, 11, 14, 15, 18, 20, 22, 23, 24, 25, 26 (twig frame): photka/shutterstock.com • 2–3 (textile): scyther5/shutterstock.com • 2, 21, 32 (frame of wooden twigs): Basileus/shutterstock.com • 4 (checkered tablecloth): Andrey_Kuzmin/shutterstock.com
4 (paper plate): Mega Pixel/shutterstock.com • 6, 14, 15, 23, 30–31 (canvas texture): Polina Katritch/shutterstock.com • 8, 16 (fabric texture): Ivanova Natalia/shutterstock.com • 17 (chocolate): Gayvoronskaya_Yana/shutterstock.com • 27 (heart of acorns): Cora Mueller/shutterstock.com